cathy cassidy

Love, Peace & Chocolate

PUFFIN

PUFFIN BOOKS

Published by the Penguin Group
Penguin Books Ltd, 80 Strand, London WC2R ORL, England
Penguin Group (USA) Inc., 375 Hudson Street, New York, New York 10014, USA
Penguin Group (Canada), 90 Eglinton Avenue East, Suite 700, Toronto, Ontario, Canada M4P 2Y3
(a division of Pearson Penguin Canada Inc.)
Penguin Ireland, 25 St Stephen's Green, Dublin 2, Ireland (a division of Penguin Books Ltd)
Penguin Group (Australia), 250 Camberwell Road, Camberwell, Victoria 3124, Australia
(a division of Pearson Australia Group Pty Ltd)
Penguin Books India Pvt Ltd, 11 Community Centre, Panchsheel Park, New Delhi – 110 017, India
Penguin Group (NZ), 67 Apollo Drive, Rosedale, North Shore 0632, New Zealand
(a division of Pearson New Zealand Ltd)
Penguin Books (South Africa) (Pty) Ltd, 24 Sturdee Avenue, Rosebank,
Johannesburg 2196, South Africa

Penguin Books Ltd, Registered Offices: 80 Strand, London WC2R ORL, England

puffinbooks.com

First published 2007
Published in this edition 2010
007

Set in Adobe Caslon 13.75/21 pt by Ellipsis Books Limited, Glasgow
Made and printed in England by Clays Ltd, St Ives plc

British Library Cataloguing in Publication Data
A CIP catalogue record for this book is available from the British Library

ISBN: 978-0-141-33021-1

www.greenpenguin.co.uk

KT 2305190 6

Cathy Cassidy wrote and illustrated her first book aged eight years old. She has worked as a fiction editor on *Jackie* magazine, an art teacher and as agony aunt on *Shout* magazine. She lives in the Scottish countryside, with her husband, two children, two cats, some mad rabbits and a mad hairy lurcher called Kelpie.

Books by Cathy Cassidy

DIZZY

INDIGO BLUE

DRIFTWOOD

SCARLETT

SUNDAE GIRL

LUCKY STAR

GINGERSNAPS

ANGEL CAKE

LETTERS TO CATHY

SHINE ON, DAIZY STAR

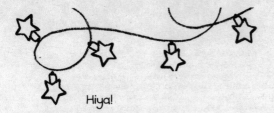

Hiya!

Love, Peace and Chocolate is a story I wrote a couple of years ago, all about friendship, chocolate - and falling for the same boy. The story came out as a free mini-book, but supplies were limited, and it has never available to buy . . . until now!

I think you'll like *Love, Peace and Chocolate*. It's one of my favourites, anyhow! It's a book that celebrates friendship, and that's something all of us should take time out to do. Friends are fab, right? They keep us going when things go pear-shaped, and they're always there to share a laugh, a secret, a dream.

Keep your friendship strong by signing up to keep the Friendship Charter on my website, *cathycassidy.com* - or check out the My Best Friend Rocks competition on the website, and tell me why your friend is so special.

I hope you enjoy *Love, Peace and Chocolate*. Seriously, what more could a girl want?

Friends forever . . .

Cathy Cassidy

xxxx

I

hey jess! dying of boredom in french, karl
williams is actually asleep on the desk.
SNORING. seriously. if i survive, meet u
in the music room at lunchtime. txt bak,
my moby's switched to silent.
love, peace & chocolate,
kady xxxx

kady, mon amie, my moby wasn't set to
silent & now i hav 100 lines to do this

lunchtime, thanks a bunch!
love, peace & chocolate,
jess x

Kady and me have been best friends – well, forever, pretty much. We met at three years old, at toddler group. Mum says Kady nicked my Playdoh, and I retaliated by chucking a bit of soggy flapjack at her. We bonded later, over the finger-paints, and we've never looked back.

We've been through a lot together, Kady and me. We braved playgroup, nursery, primary school. We discovered Bratz dolls, Brownies and ballet, and also nits, chicken-pox and verrucas. (Don't worry; those days are gone!)

Secondary school brought a whole new

bunch of stuff to handle: French verbs, Bunsen burners, equilateral triangles – and also first periods (Kady) and first bras (both of us). We're looking forward to the first love, first boyfriend, first kiss bit too, but things have been kind of slow on this score.

I don't know if we're just unlucky, but there's not a whole lot of choice at Parkway Community School. There isn't a single Year Eight boy who can make my heart beat faster – except for Karl Williams that time he set off a firework right outside Mr Barrow's science class, and that was only because I thought it was a terrorist attack. Maybe it's because we've known these boys since primary, or maybe they're just exceptionally plain, charmless and downright annoying.

'One day,' Kady sighs, peering out of the

window at Karl Williams and his gang, who are playing football with an old tin can in the pouring rain. 'One day, we'll meet a couple of cute, cool lads. Just you wait!'

'Not in this school, we won't.'

We're in the music room. Miss Anderson lets us hang out in here because I'm meant to be practising my flute for her, but there hasn't been a whole lot of practice going on lately. I pick up my flute and run through a couple of scales to keep the guilt at bay, then scrawl another few lines of *I must not leave my mobile phone switched on during lesson time*.

'So,' says Kady. 'Talking of cute, cool lads ... Who would you rather kiss? Mr Barrow, Karl Williams or ... a frog?'

'Oh, gross!' I protest. 'Not Mr Barrow –

he's got to be at least sixty, and those nylon shirts he wears . . .'

'Tasteful,' Kady smirks.

'Scary,' I correct her. 'And Karl Williams? No way! Nope, it'd have to be the frog.'

'Even though it's fat and slimy and covered in warts?' Kady demands.

'Even though,' I admit. 'It's the best option of the three, by far. And who knows, if I kiss it, it might turn into a handsome prince!'

'You're a dreamer,' Kady tells me. 'There are no princes any more. There are no cool boys at Parkway, full stop – I think they screen them out and pack them all off to private schools to stop them from distracting us. We could grow old and grey and shrivelled and never be kissed, the way things are going.'

'Rubbish,' I tell her. 'You're so impatient,

Kady! We're twelve years old. That's not exactly old and grey and shrivelled.'

'No – they're the best years of our lives, my mum reckons,' Kady says. 'We've got it all, according to her. Clear skin, skinny hips, shiny hair, endless energy. And what are we doing? Wasting it all on lines and flute practice. That's sad.'

'Well, the lines bit is kind of your fault.'

'I said I was sorry!' she huffs. 'Look, this is serious, Jess! What do we want from life? Love, peace and chocolate. Not much to ask, is it?'

'We can usually manage the chocolate bit,' I say reasonably.

Kady thumps the tabletop. 'It's not enough!' she argues. 'What about peace? No more war, no more hunger, no more maths homework?'

'I don't know if a ban on homework would actually help with world peace,' I say.

'Of course it would,' Kady scoffs. She runs a comb through my hair, twists it into a wispy little bun and pins it by my ear. 'And what about *love*? What about romance? Don't you ever feel that life is passing you by?'

'You have to be patient,' I tell her. 'You can't rush fate!'

'Dream on!' Kady scoffs. 'Fate's just for fairy stories, Jess. There are no princes, only frogs, and fate is another word for do-as-you're-told. Face it, if we sit around here waiting for Prince Charming to show up, we'll still be here when we're ninety.'

'So what are we gonna do instead?' I ask.

'Get out there and grab life with both

hands,' Kady announces. 'I suppose. Some day.'

Kady finishes messing with my hair and shows me the result in a hand mirror. She has pinned up two tiny, twisty little buns on either side of my face. It's cute, if a little weird, like something an elf-queen might wear in one of those *Lord of the Rings* films.

Kady is fab at hairstyles – she's been practising on me since we were six years old, so she should be. She wears her own hair in tight, beaded braids pretty much all of the time, because otherwise it goes fluffy and frizzy. It always looks amazing, though – it complements her smooth, latte-coffee skin just perfectly.

'Like it?' Kady wants to know.

'Love it. Thanks, Kady!'

She grabs up the lined paper and swipes my pen. 'I'll finish these for you,' she says. 'After all, like you said, it was partly my fault too. You practise, OK?'

She leans over the lined paper, scribbling furiously, and I pick up my flute and play.

I love to play the flute – and Kady, for all her joking around, loves to listen. She even put up with me in the days when my playing was more like the screeching you'd get if you stood on a cat's tail, but now, after four years of practice, I can actually hold a tune.

When I play, it's all about breath and concentration and cold, shiny silver for a while – and then all of that falls away and it's just music, clear, cool music, chasing away the rain and the homework, the hassles, the drudgery.

The notes rise up, filling the scuddy old classroom with light, shimmering into the darkest corners, flying like birds up through the ceiling and onwards, right up into the sky.

Then it's over, and I lower my flute and take a breath in, grinning at Kady, who has abandoned the lines, gone all sad-eyed and dreamy.

'Lovely,' she sighs.

And then there's a soft, slow clapping from the back of the room, and a tall, slim boy steps out of the shadows.

'Yeah,' he says. 'That was . . . awesome!'

Kady turns to look, and I can see her eyes open wide, her jaw drop, her cheeks flush softly with pink. Me – I'm just about crimson.

'Didn't mean to embarrass you,' he says.

'I just didn't want to interrupt, y'know? I don't usually like classical music, but that was something else!'

The boy in the shadows is tall and smiley. He's wearing an old black suit jacket covered with band badges, low-slung cords and a skinny black jumper, and on his back is a black guitar case, slung diagonally across his body. As we gawp, he walks lazily across the room, shrugs the guitar case off and leans it against the wall.

'Miss Anderson said I could leave it here till later,' he grins.

The bell rings out then, signalling the end of lunchbreak, and Kady jumps up, smooths her skirt down, finds her voice.

'Um . . . we don't know you, do we?' she says. 'You don't go to Parkway, do you?'

The boy laughs, shaking a mess of choppy, caramel-coloured hair out of his sparkly dark blue eyes. 'Yeah, I go to Parkway,' he says. 'As of three days ago, anyhow! My folks just came down here from Liverpool. I'm still settling in, I guess. I'm in Year Nine.'

'I'm Kady Hamilton and this is Jess Taylor,' Kady says, twisting one long, beaded braid around her finger. 'We're Year Eight. And you are . . .?'

He slips his thumbs through the belt-loops of his skinny cords and tilts his head to one side.

'Jack,' he says, looking right at me. 'I'm Jack Somers.'

2

jess, i take it all bak, wot i said about
fate. jack somers IS my fate, ok? he is SO
cool!!!!
love, peace & chocolate,
kady xxxx

kady, d'u no wot time it is? 3 in the
morning! yeah, jack's cool, yeah, he's cute.
i'm mad about him 2, but rite now i need
2 sleep. i'm switchin my moby off.

seriously.
love, peace & chocolate,
jess zzzz

Kady waits for me at the bus stop in a black, pleated skirt short enough to stop traffic and a tight black tank top instead of the regulation sweatshirt over her crisp white shirt. Her eyes are rimmed with black eyeliner, and her lips glisten with strawberry lipgloss.

The bus rolls up and we pile on, squash in at the back.

'You look amazing,' I tell Kady. 'I wish I'd known we were dressing up – I feel kind of boring next to you!'

'No way!' Kady says. 'You're great! You've got that dreamy, other-worldly look – boys love that! C'mon, Jack already thinks you're dead talented and cool. I can't compete with that, but – well, I don't want him to think I'm childish or anything, y'know?'

'He won't!' I tell her. 'You look fourteen at least. He'll go crazy for you!'

'No, it's you he likes,' Kady insists. 'Lucky thing!'

'No way,' I protest, although I secretly hope that she's right. 'He's out of our league, but we can dream, can't we? I mean . . . that boy is SO cute!!!'

'Gorgeous,' Kady breathes. 'Did you see those eyes? That hair?'

'How about his clothes?' I chip in. 'He's just so cool! And he plays guitar! He's probably in a band!'

The bus shudders to a halt and we spill out on to the pavement outside the school gates, just as the nine o'clock bell peals out.

'I think I'm in love,' Kady sighs.

'Me too.'

We link arms and mooch off to registration, dreaming of Jack Somers.

By breaktime, Kady has gathered a whole raft of information about Jack. His tutor group is 9C, based in room 43, and his favourite subjects are English, art and music. He used to have a band back in Liverpool, and he'd like to start one here. And guess what? Half the girls in the school are crazy about him already. More than half, really – the others just haven't admitted it yet.

'We don't stand a chance,' I tell Kady. 'We're only Year Eights. Why would he look at us?'

Kady raises one perfect, black-winged eyebrow. 'Why wouldn't he?' she asks. 'Trust me, Jess. I have a feeling about this. It's like you said – fate.'

Sure enough, when we head into the music room at lunchtime, Jack Somers is sprawled at a desk in the corner, cutting random mismatched letters from an old newspaper. Sheets of black A3 paper, Pritt Stick and a mound of little silver stars are sprinkled across the desktop.

'Oh, hi,' says Kady carelessly. 'Jack, isn't it?'

'Hi, Kady,' he grins. 'Hi, Jess.'

Is it my imagination, or does he hold my gaze a moment longer than he has to? Those dark blue eyes make my insides turn to slush, make my fingers tremble.

'What are you up to?' Kady wants to know,

sitting on the edge of his desk. 'What are you making? Ransom notes?'

Jack arranges the cut-out letters carefully on the black paper, spelling out the words *Fallen Stars*.

'I'm starting a band,' he tells us. 'Fallen Stars. Miss Anderson says I can hold auditions in the music room after school on Friday, so I'm doing some posters. Want to help?'

'OK!'

We sit with Jack all lunchtime, sticking snipped-out letters on to black card, spelling out the name of the band, the date, place and time of the auditions. We talk about his favourite bands – The View, The Fratellis, The Kooks, Razorlight – the names on the button badges that cover his lapels. We talk about Parkway Community School and

Fallen Stars and Liverpool and fame. Jack takes a bar of Fruit & Nut from his pocket and shares it out, and I pocket the blue foil paper secretly, because it was Jack's, and I think I might keep it forever.

Five minutes before the bell goes, we sprinkle confetti stars all over the posters and Jack tells us they look totally awesome.

'Do you two play anything?' he asks us. 'Well, I know you do, Jess, but a flute's not really the right kind of instrument for a rock band. D'you play anything else? Bass guitar, keyboards, drums?'

'Just flute,' I admit.

'OK,' says Jack. 'Never mind.'

'We could help out at the auditions, though,' Kady says. 'You know, making a note of anyone you wanted to see again, their names and forms and stuff. And we could help put these posters up!'

'Would you?' Jack grins. 'That'd be fantastic! I'd really appreciate it.'

'No hassle,' Kady shrugs, still playing it cool. 'It'll be a laugh. See you around, Jack, OK?'

'OK,' he says. 'And thanks!'

Kady links her arm through mine and we head for the door.

'Wow,' she whispers, the minute we get outside. 'Wow! I can't believe it, can you? Did you see his badge?'

'Which one?' I ask, because there have to be a dozen button badges stuck to the lapels of Jack's black jacket.

'Which one?' Kady echoes. 'The CND

badge, of course! The peace badge! Can you believe it?'

'Um . . . well, he seems kind of cool, so yeah, why not?' I say, puzzled.

'And the chocolate?' Kady says. 'He had chocolate in his bag . . .'

'So? Everyone loves chocolate,' I frown.

'Don't you get it?' Kady laughs. 'Don't you see, Jess? He's perfect! He's perfect for *us*! The peace badge, the chocolate bar . . . love, peace and chocolate!'

'Right,' I say. 'OK. What about love, then?'

Kady rolls her eyes and shakes her beautiful braids. 'Jess,' she says, hands on hips. 'Do you really have to ask?'

3

hey jess! hav u finished yr maths hw?
can't settle. can i come round?
love, peace & chocolate,
kady xxx

kady – get marshmallows from the corner
shop & i'll put the kettle on. don't b
long!!!!
love, peace & chocolate,
jess x

We're holed up in my room, sipping hot chocolate and melted marshmallows with chocolate flakes dipped in.

'I can't stop thinking about him,' Kady tells me. 'Seriously. It's like an illness. At school, at home, when I'm working, when I'm eating, when I'm sleeping.'

'I know,' I say. 'It's scary. I don't like it.'

'I do,' Kady argues. 'It's like I've never really been alive before, y'know? And now every single bit of me tingles every time I think of him. I feel like I could fly!'

'It's more like an ache all around your heart,' I tell her. 'Plus butterflies in your stomach, and shivers all up and down your spine!'

'Sounds like indigestion with a bit of flu thrown in,' Kady laughs. 'We're in a bad way, both of us. And there's no cure – no cure except Jack!'

We sip our hot chocolates.

'You know what's really weird about this?' I say eventually. 'We both want Jack. It's a bit like when we were seven and we both wanted Furbies for Christmas – remember? And all the shops had run out. In the end you got a grey one and I got a pink one, so we were both happy. Only this time . . .'

'There's only one Jack.'

'Well, yeah.'

I dig my toybox out from under the bed, pick out the old pink Furby. It's hard to imagine feeling so strongly about a scrap of fur fabric with a few wires inside, but I did. And when Mum let slip that Kady's nan had found a Furby for her in a shop in

Manchester, I was sick with jealousy. I didn't want Kady to have what I couldn't have.

Of course, in the end Dad found me one too, when he was on a business trip to London, so everything worked out fine. This time, though, things could turn out differently.

'We can't both have Jack,' Kady says.

'Maybe neither of us will,' I shrug. 'He's probably so dedicated to his music he doesn't have time for girlfriends. Or maybe he already has someone back in Liverpool?'

'Hope not,' Kady frowns. 'I tell you one thing, though – if he's going to have a girlfriend, and it's not me . . . well, I hope it's you, OK?'

'Seriously?'

'Seriously!' Kady says. 'I mean, he'd have

to be crazy to pass up the chance to date me, but hey, perhaps the guy's short-sighted . . .'

I swat her with a pillow until she squeals and shrieks and begs for mercy, and we end up tickling each other and giggling and promising to be friends forever.

'You're so cool and clever and unusual-looking,' Kady tells me. 'And you've already bewitched him with your flute-playing. Jack's going to fall for you, for sure.'

'No, he'll go for you,' I argue. 'He'd be nuts not to. You could be a model, Kady, with your dark eyes and your amazing skin and that wonderful hair. How could he resist?'

'It could be one of us, Jess,' she says softly. 'Why not?'

I pick up the old pink Furby, stroke its fur dreamily. 'One of us, though,' I say. 'How weird would that be? Because even if Jack does fall for one of us . . . well, it's exactly that. One of us. Not both.'

'Well, I hope it's you,' Kady says loyally.

'And I hope it's you,' I echo, even though I'm not entirely sure that I do. 'It would feel kind of strange, though, if he asked you out. I don't know how I'd handle that.'

'You'd be happy for me,' Kady says confidently. 'And I'd be happy for you, if it was the other way around. That's what friendship is all about. No boy is ever going to come between us. Right?'

'Right.'

'Best friends forever,' Kady tells me. 'No matter what.'

We lie back, eating the rest of the marshmallows and listening to The View so we can be sussed and knowledgeable in front of Jack.

'Sometimes,' I whisper, 'I can't work out whether Jack is the best thing that ever happened to us, or the worst. He's something else, y'know? Scary!'

'Tell me about it,' Kady sighs. 'He's been at Parkway – what – a week? Already he's turned everything upside down. He's like a firework or something.'

'Light blue touchpaper and stand well back,' I say, quoting from the box of rockets and fountains Dad bought last Bonfire Night.

'Exactly,' says Kady. 'Only who wants to stand on the sidelines when they could get a little bit closer? See the magic close up?'

That's what's happening with Kady and me – we know we should stay back, but we can't resist. We don't care about the danger.

We don't care that we'll get our fingers burnt.

Us and about a million other Parkway girls.

4

hey jess, audition day! shall i wear my
black combats or the little skirt with the
frill? boots or sk8 shoes? can i borrow yr
Razorlight badge?
love, peace & chocolate,
kady xoxox

hi kady. combats, deffy, and sk8 shoes —
we want 2 look cool, not glam. i'll bring
the badge, & chocolate for courage. c u at

the bus stop.
love, peace & chocolate,
jess x

Of course, Kady manages to look glam anyway. She's wearing her combats so low a sliver of black thong appears at the back whenever she bends down or stretches up. A thong? I didn't know Kady possessed such a thing. My mum still buys me pastel cartoon-print knickers from the kids' section at Tesco, the kind that come right up to your armpits, just about.

Next to Kady, I feel colourless, dull, like a favourite top that ran in the wash and came out all faded and grey.

There's a sizzle of excitement in the air, like something cool is just about to happen.

Word has got out that Kady and I are helping with the auditions, and kids are asking us if they can come and watch.

'No, sorry, it's strictly business,' Kady tells them. 'Fallen Stars will be playing a whole bunch of gigs later in the term, but right now things are top secret. Musicians only! If you play an instrument, I can take your name and allot you a time . . .'

'Can I audition to be the band's personal stylist?' one girl asks.

'Does Jack *look* like he needs a personal stylist?' Kady says witheringly, and the girl turns away, crushed.

Then we see Karl Williams. He's flattened his usually spiky hair into a tousled Jack-style, couldn't-care-less cut, and swapped his trademark mud-spattered joggers for black cord hipsters. They're so low they may be in danger of falling down, and he has to pause every couple of steps to yank them upwards.

'Did we really see that?' I ask Kady, as we reach the sanctuary of the lockers and collapse on each other with squeals and guffaws. 'Was it real?'

'Think so,' Kady splutters. 'Karl Williams gets cool! How weird is that?'

'D'you think he's auditioning?' I giggle. 'I never knew Karl Williams was a musician! What d'you think he plays?'

'The triangle?' Kady suggests. 'The comb and paper?'

'It's Jack,' I muse. 'Ever since he arrived at Parkway, the place has gone crazy. All the girls are mad about him, all the boys want to be like him. Even the teachers act like he's something special.'

'Well,' says Kady. 'He is.'

Auditions are due to start at three thirty, in the music room. Miss Anderson has set up drums, keyboard, guitars, mikes and amps, and Kady is herding people in, checking names off on a clipboard. Pretty soon there are kids sitting on the tables, kids sitting on the window sills, kids sitting on the floor. They fill up every bit of the room until it's like a sardine can, with kids shoehorned in everywhere you look.

At three forty, Jack lopes into the room, tall and skinny and smiley, guitar in hand. He steps up to the mike, and right away you can tell that he belongs there. The room is silent.

'Thanks for coming along,' Jack says. 'I know I'm new to Parkway, but I'm not new to music – I've been writing songs and playing in bands for five years now. It's my life. I asked you along here today because I want to find people I can work with, people who love music the same way I do. I want to find my new band – Fallen Stars!'

A ragged round of applause flares up, Kady ushers the first few kids forward and the auditions begin. It doesn't take long to whittle down the applicants. Kady is ruthless – she weeds out the trumpeters, the saxophonists, the clarinettists, the Year Seven girls who turned up clutching recorders and batting their eyelashes. She gets rid of a speccy boy with a cello and a couple of chancers with a tambourine.

The Year Nine girls wearing micro-minis and shirts knotted up to show their bellies are way harder to shift.

'What do you play?' I ask them, pencil poised over my clipboard.

'We'll play whatever Jack wants us to play,' the blonde one smirks. 'We're very talented.'

My cheeks flood with colour. 'What instrument?' I ask again.

The blonde girl rolls her eyes. 'We're the backing singers,' she huffs. 'And we dance, too. Jack knows all about us. He asked us along, personally.'

'Right. Um . . .'

'What's up?' Jack calls over, raking a hand through his hair.

'Backing singers,' I tell him. 'Shall I ask them to wait?'

'We're a rock band,' he shouts over. 'No backing singers. Sorry, girls!' He turns away.

The blonde girl raises an eyebrow at me, letting her eyes skim over my dull school uniform, my shiny shoes. 'What do you play?' she asks. 'Oh, yeah, I know. Make-believe . . .'

Well, maybe I do. I make-believe that I belong in this music room, and I make-believe that Jack is my boyfriend. I make-believe I'm useful, checking names off my list, adjusting the sound levels when the amps go haywire, fixing a guitar when a scary Year Eleven goth snaps three strings doing a painful Marilyn Manson solo.

I even make-believe that I don't care when this blonde would-be backing singer looks at me like I'm something nasty she just wiped off the sole of her kitten-heeled boot.

'Hey, gorgeous,' a voice says, and Karl Williams slips an arm around the blonde girl, towing her towards the door. 'You're definitely the best backing singers we've seen, so if Jack changes his mind, you'll be the first to know . . .'

'Who are you, then?' she asks.

'I'm in the band,' Karl says smoothly. 'Jack's kind of busy right now, getting the line-up right, but I'll be sure to put in a good word for you girls later . . .'

He shoves them gently through the door, shuts it firmly, then turns to me, grinning.

'Thanks,' I say.

'Any time,' he grins. 'So . . . any chance

you can get me up to the top of that list of yours? I'm the best drummer here. Jack needs me.'

'Yeah, right,' I laugh.

But when Karl Williams picks up the drumsticks and belts out a frantic drum roll, everyone stops talking to listen. 'That's cool,' Jack says. 'You're good. Stick around, Karl – you're in!'

Bit by bit, the room empties until there are just a few kids left. A Year Nine lad gets the slot of bass guitarist, and an elfin Year Ten girl gets to do the keyboards. They start jamming together, getting used to each other, ending up with a wild version of Jet's 'Are You Gonna Be My Girl?'.

I'm good enough at make-believe to imagine Jack's singing for me, but one look at Kady tells me she's thinking the same thing, and my heart takes a dive.

Who am I kidding? Not even myself.

5

jess, can u believe it? we hav a date with
jack somers! don't let me faint or tell him
that i love him, & if my knees start
shaking, just kick me!
 love, peace & chocolate,
 kady xxxx

kady, it's rude 2 txt when yr with the boy
of yr dreams. calm down — & switch yr
moby off, ok?

love, peace & chocolate,
jess x

'What's with the texting?' Jack wants to know. 'Parents want to know where you are?'

'That's right,' Kady says. 'Jess has very strict parents. They're always texting to check she's not out on the town with some gorgeous lad when she should be at home with her flute.'

'Kady!' I protest, blushing crimson.

'Joke!' Kady laughs. 'Jess has lovely parents, seriously.'

Jack looks at Kady like he can't quite work her out. I know the feeling – I've been trying to work her out since I was three years old, and I'm still no further forward. Of course, it's just possible Jack is admiring the shrinkto-fit *rock chick* T-shirt and the little black skirt.

'Like the look,' I whisper to Kady. 'What is it, Year Nine backing singer?'

'You're just jealous,' she whispers back.

Well – yeah.

'I wanted to say thanks for all your help with the auditions,' Jack is saying. 'I never really know what to say to the no-hopers, or the kids who have talent but play the wrong instruments. You took care of all that stuff. You were smart and kind and ultra-organized. You even restrung that guitar, Jess! So . . . I wanted to take you both for a meal, say thanks properly. Where d'you fancy?'

'The local pizza place is OK,' Kady says. 'You'd like it, Jack. They do great chocolate cake, too!'

'OK,' grins Jack. 'That sounds like a plan!'

We grab a window table in the pizza place and order a margherita with extra pineapple, olives and anchovies, just to see what it's like. Then we discover that anchovies are fish, and Kady says that's gross, so we pick them all off, one by one.

'I'm so glad I met you two,' Jack is saying, his dark blue eyes twinkling as he munches pizza. 'You have dodgy taste in pizza, but you've been real mates.'

'Any time,' Kady says. 'You've been pretty cool yourself.'

'I can't wait to start working with the new band,' Jack says. 'That kid on the drums is something else.'

'You can say that again,' Kady mutters.

'He's OK,' I chip in, remembering how he

rescued me from the stroppy backing singers.

'Karl, isn't it?' Jack says. 'And Lucie on keyboards, Alex on bass.'

'It's a great line-up, Jack,' I tell him. 'You're going to be brilliant. Loads of kids have been asking when you'll be playing gigs!'

'Hey, I should make you two my managers,' he grins. 'I love the music bit, but I'm hopeless when it comes to the rest of it.'

'Stick with us,' Kady says. 'We'll make you rich and famous! Fancy playing at the summer-term disco?'

'I'll give it a go,' Jack shrugs.

'Or . . . well, maybe we could do better than that,' I say. 'I mean, you have a bit of a following already, and if that Jet song was anything to go by, you're going to be pretty good by the time you've got used to each other, had some practice. Maybe we could do a festival, a kind of benefit gig?'

'Outside,' Kady says slowly. 'On the school playing fields. Like Glastonbury, but at Parkway!'

'We could sell tickets, raise money for . . . I don't know, famine victims in Africa, or that charity that campaigns against landmines,' I suggest. 'The kids would love it, and even the teachers would have to approve. We could call it . . . Parkway Peace Festival!'

Jack is looking at me like he never really noticed me before, like I'm the most wonderful person he ever met in his life. 'Awesome,' he breathes.

I know he means the idea, and not me personally, but still, my heart starts to race. It's a good feeling – a great feeling.

Then Kady leans across, presses a napkin into my hand. 'Jess,' she whispers. 'You've got mozzarella on your chin.'

I will never eat pizza again. How stupid can you get? You think a boy is looking into your eyes, hanging on your every word, but actually he's trying to work out how to tell you you just dropped your dinner all down your chin. Yuk.

By the time the chocolate cake arrives, I'm back in the shadows. Jack and Kady are talking about the peace festival, adding new ideas, scribbling plans on the back of an unused napkin. Their heads are close together, glossy black braids and choppy caramel. They look good together. They look like they belong.

'We could do stalls,' Jack is saying. 'Face-painting, that kind of thing . . .'

'We could make a giant dreamcatcher and get everyone to write their dreams on to ribbons and tie them on!' Kady offers.

'Nice one. How about drumming work-shops? Karl could get that one organized. And stilt-walkers, and jugglers, and a dance tent! What d'you think, Jess?'

'Fine,' I say, but nobody's listening.

It's dark when we spill out on to the pave-ment, and Kady hooks her arm through Jack's, huddles in. I hold back, let them go on ahead. I wish the ground could open up and swallow me, because now I can see that three is a crowd. I'm the odd one out. Then Jack turns back, holding out his other arm.

'C'mon, Jess!' he grins. 'You've got those

faraway eyes again! Stop dreaming! Let's go!'

I take his arm, do as he says.

I stop dreaming. Hope falls away from me like pine needles off a Christmas tree in January. There's a cold, sad ache inside me, and it won't go away.

6

jess, y won't u answer my txts? i just
HAV 2 talk 2 u . . . i'm so HAPPY! u'll
neva guess wot happened after we left u.
like i said, it's fate! c u at the bus stop.
love, peace & chocolate,
kady xxxxxxxxxxxxxxx

kady, not feeling well. gonna leave my
moby off & sleep.

love, peace & chocolate,
jess

'Are you sure you don't want me to take you to the doctor's?' Mum says, hovering in the doorway with a mug of hot lemon. 'There's been a nasty bug going round. Maybe they can do something?'

'Nobody can do anything,' I groan. 'It's probably just one of those twenty-four-hour things. I'll be better tomorrow.'

'Well, OK,' Mum says uncertainly. 'I just wish I didn't have to work today. Stay in bed, pet; I'll call the school and explain. Drink this – it might just help. And call me if you feel any worse, OK?'

'OK. Bye, Mum.'

I hear the front door click, and I pull the duvet over my head. I think I might die, seriously, but it's not something a doctor can help me with and it's not something that sleep or hot lemon can cure. My heart feels heavy, so heavy I can't see how I can ever stand up and walk around again.

Kady and Jack. Even their names sound good together, like they were meant to be. Why didn't I see that from the start? I could have stopped myself from hoping, stopped myself from dreaming.

Then I remember how it felt when Jack looked at me, smiled at me, and I know that I was always going to hope, no matter what.

I pick up my mobile, flick to the in-box, scroll through Kady's messages from last night, this morning. Fifteen texts, fifteen different ways of telling me something I just don't want to know.

'. . . gotta talk 2 u, jess, u'll neva believe it . . .'

'. . . something wonderful, AMAZING, fantastic, awesome . . .'

'. . . i no yr gonna be happy 4 me, jess, i just no it . . .'

Well, no, sorry, Kady, I'm not.

I shut my eyes and let the tears come, hot, burning tears of self-pity. I want something I can't have – I want Jack. He saw me first, after all – he walked out of the shadows and looked into my eyes and told me my flute-playing was awesome, and it was the first time ever a boy looked at me like I was somebody cool, somebody cute, somebody interesting. And all the time, he wanted Kady.

'Jess? How are you feeling?'

Someone tugs at the curtains, letting a sliver of daylight into the room, and I moan and burrow deeper into my pillow. My head aches and there's a stale, sour taste in my mouth.

'Jess? I bought some stuff to cheer you up – chocolate and oranges and a magazine. D'you feel any better?'

It's Kady. Kady knows where we keep our spare back-door key, under the plant pot with the little blue flowers in. She's a good friend, the kind who worries when you're ill and calls into the shops on her way home to buy you oranges and chocolate and your favourite magazine.

I'm a bad friend, the kind who wants to throw those things right back at her, scream, shout, tell her to get out of my house and never come back.

I don't, though. I sit up carefully, hugging the duvet around me, rubbing my eyes. 'Thanks, Kady,' I say. 'You didn't have to.'

'So are you any better?' she wants to know. 'What is it, a cold?'

'Just one of those twenty-four-hour things, I think,' I tell her. 'You know, aches and pains and fever and sickness. It's not so bad now.'

'Your eyes look all red, too,' Kady says. 'Poor you.'

Yeah, poor me.

Kady huddles up on the bed, peels an orange and splits it in half. 'Eat it,' she insists. 'It's good for you. Vitamin C.'

'Thanks.'

'I thought you'd gone a bit quiet last night,' she muses. 'You must have been feeling rotten.'

'Well, a bit,' I admit.

'Um – you know after we left you, me and Jack?' Kady says. 'After we dropped you at your house and headed on to mine?'

'Mmm?'

'Well – look, Jess, I don't know how to say this.'

So don't, I think, but of course she does anyway.

'We were talking for a bit outside my gate, and then . . . Jack kissed me. He kissed me,

56

Jess! Then he asked me out! Can you believe it?'

I take a deep breath in, biting the inside of my cheek until I taste blood. 'Wow,' I say shakily. 'That's great, Kady.'

'You're OK with it?' Kady's eyes light up like Christmas lights and her lips curve into a big, happy grin. 'Oh, Jess, I was so worried you'd be hurt or angry or something. I mean, I know we said that no boy would ever come between us – I'd drop him in a minute if I thought you had a problem with all this – but, well, it's *Jack*. I've never met a boy like him before.'

'No,' I echo.

'He's special,' Kady says.

'I know,' I whisper.

'So. That's it, then, really. I wanted to tell

you face to face, know that you were OK with it all. Oh, Jess, I'm so glad you understand – I couldn't turn him down, I just couldn't, you know?'

'I know,' I tell her. 'It's OK, really.'

'Nothing's going to change,' Kady says, but she's wrong about that, I know. Everything is different now.

It may never be the same again.

7

hey jess, thanx 4 being so cool about jack.
yr the best friend eva! told miss Anderson
about your festival idea and she's going to
ask the head. fingers crossed!
love, peace & chocolate,
kady xxxx

that's great about the festival. and
seriously, kady, if anyone deserves jack it's
gotta b u. i'm happy 4 u, really.

love, peace & chocolate,
jess x

Lies drip off my tongue like ice cream. No, I'm not happy for Kady. No, I don't think she deserves Jack. Not really. If I can't have him, why should she? I'm jealous, pure and simple, except that there's nothing pure and nothing simple about it.

Sometimes, I guess, the truth is something you just have to keep to yourself.

I'd like to tell Kady how I feel. I'd like to see her face fall, watch her try to talk her way out of this one. She said she'd ditch Jack in a minute if I wasn't happy about the two of them, but talk's easy. Would she do it? I don't think so. I wouldn't, I know, if things were the other way round.

Y'see, Jack's too good to be true. It's like if you paid 10p for a lucky dip and came up with an iPod when everyone else was stuck with penny sweets and plastic whistles. You wouldn't exactly hand it back and say it wasn't fair, would you? It's the luck of the draw.

It's not Kady's fault, not really. She just got lucky, and I didn't, and I can't tell her how I feel because then I'll lose her, as well as Jack. Instead I paste a fake smile on to my face and pretend everything is fine, and the lies just keep on coming.

'No, of course I don't mind if you see Jack this Saturday. Why would I?'

We're in Kady's room, supposedly revising for a history test, but the only dates Kady has mentioned so far are dates with Jack.

'Well, we usually hang out together on a Saturday, that's all,' Kady says.

'I know, but that was before,' I shrug. 'Things can't stay the same forever.'

I lean back against the wall, listening to the new compilation CD Jack made for Kady. The Fratellis are singing that a girl like me's *just irresistible*, which is kind of ironic.

'We'll make it another night, then,' Kady says. 'By the way, Miss Anderson wants us to put some plans on paper for the Parkway Peace Festival. It looks like it could really happen!'

'I know. I never thought they'd actually go for it!'

'Maybe we should all meet up and brainstorm ideas again?' Kady suggests. 'You and me and Jack.'

'No way,' I say, a little too quickly. 'I don't want to tag along on your dates, thank you!'

'It wouldn't be like that,' Kady says. 'We're all friends, aren't we?'

'We were,' I correct her. 'Not now. It'd be kind of awkward for me.'

'I don't see why,' Kady frowns. 'Jack wouldn't mind.'

'I'd mind.'

'Well, I suppose you might feel a bit left out. Jack suggested we double-date sometime, if you'd like to,' Kady tells me. 'That'd be cool, wouldn't it?'

About as cool as having your toenails pulled out one by one with red-hot pliers. Watching your best mate and the boy you're crazy about together? No thanks.

'What if Jack hooked you up with Alex

out of the band?' Kady says. 'That might be interesting! He's cute!'

'Not my type,' I say lightly.

'No? Well, how about Karl Williams and his magic drumsticks? Tasty!'

'Don't laugh at him,' I say. 'Poor Karl!'

'Poor Karl? C'mon, Jess. You once said you'd rather kiss a frog!'

I let out a long, exasperated breath.

'Right now I wouldn't want to kiss any-body,' I say, which is such a big, fat lie my tongue will probably turn black. 'Think of all those germs.'

'Oh, Jess,' Kady sighs. She gives me a pitying look, like I'm about six years old and don't know anything. 'It's not like that. Kissing's just . . . well, wonderful. You'll understand, one day.'

Then I get mad, because maybe, if it wasn't for Kady, I'd understand right now. Maybe Jack would have hung around talking outside my gate. Maybe he'd have kissed *me*, asked *me* out. Maybe.

'Don't get sulky,' Kady says.

'I'm not.'

'You are. I was only saying . . .'

'Well, don't!' I snap. 'I'm fed up with hearing about Jack Somers every minute of every day, OK? It's boring. *He's* boring. And you know what, Kady? You're boring, too!'

I grab up my jacket, snatch my history folder and stalk out of the room, slamming the door so hard it makes the CD jump. 'I hate you, Kady Hamilton,' I shout as I run down the stairs. 'D'you know that? I hate you! I hate you, I hate you, I HATE you!'

8

jess, u don't really hate me, do u? wot
happened 2 friends 4eva?
love, peace & chocolate,
kady xxxx

I press Delete.

For the first time ever, I have nothing to say to Kady. She's always been there for me before. She's always known the right things to say, the right things to do. She could fix anything with a grin and a hug and a bar of chocolate, but right now, she's the problem.

She's seeing Jack Somers, and I just can't stand it.

I know I shouldn't let it get to me. I should shrug off the hurt, get over it, tell myself that all's fair in love and war. I should accept the situation, but I just can't.

It's eating me up.

'Jess?' Mum says, holding up a scrap of pink fur fabric stained with tea leaves and potato peelings and stale orange juice. 'Jess, I was taking the rubbish out and I found your old Furby in the dustbin. You didn't really mean to throw it away, surely?'

I roll my eyes, curl my lip. 'Mum, I grew out of that old thing years ago.'

'Well, maybe, but you used to really love it!'

'Things change, Mum,' I say coldly. 'It's time to let go, move on.'

Mum brushes the tea leaves from the stained pink fur, wraps the toy in a shroud of kitchen roll. 'Sure?' she asks doubtfully.

'Sure,' I say.

At school, things are just as weird. I have other friends, of course I do, but they all look at me like I'm seriously insane when I tell them I'm through with Kady.

'Not really,' Ellie Bennetts says, when I sit next to her in the lunch hall. 'You might have fallen out, but you'll make up. Give it time.'

'I've wasted enough time on Kady Hamilton,' I argue. 'She's changed, Ellie.

68

She's mean and thoughtless. She doesn't care who she hurts.'

'Kady?' Ellie blinks, tucking a strand of light brown hair behind a bright, butterfly hairclip. 'No way. She's really upset about all this.'

'Don't let her fool you,' I say. 'All she cares about is Jack Somers.'

'You can't fall out over a boy,' Ellie says. 'Not you two. It's crazy! Boys come and go, but friendship is forever.'

'Not this one.'

Even so, there's a hole in my life where Kady used to be. She has been my best friend for so long, it's hard to plug up all the gaps now that she's gone. I eat my lunch with Ellie, go ice-skating with Jade and Lisa, meet Sian and Becca in town for a coffee, but it's not the same. I miss Kady, every single day.

She texts sometimes, telling me she misses *me*, asking if we can talk, and sometimes I kid myself that we could do that, work something out. Then I catch a glimpse of Jack Somers loping along the corridor with his rock-star clothes and his tousled hair and his dark blue eyes, and my heart hardens.

I delete Kady's texts, every one.

'Jess, can I talk to you a minute?' Miss Anderson ambushes me at the end of class, just as I'm packing up my stuff.

'Yes, Miss?'

'Kady's been telling me that this whole Peace Festival concept was your idea. Is that right?'

'Well, kind of,' I admit. 'I suppose.'

'It's a terrific idea,' Miss Anderson gushes. 'There's so much to arrange and organize, though, and I wondered why you weren't coming along to the meetings. We'd love you to get involved, Jess. We need your ideas. You'd have so much to contribute!'

'I can't,' I mutter.

'Can't?'

'It's awkward. It's Kady and Jack's idea now, and I've fallen out with Kady.'

Miss Anderson looks thoughtful. 'I see,' she says. 'I thought it might be something like that. You have to rise above it, Jess – the Peace Festival is too important. It's the most exciting thing we've ever tried at Parkway, in my opinion. It matters!'

'I know,' I shrug.

'We're going to run it during the day on the last week of term, and invite along all of Parkway's feeder schools,' Miss Anderson pushes on. 'Kady and Jack are involved in the music side of it, mainly, but there's much more to it than that. We're running art, drama and music workshops, stalls, events. We want to get every child involved, every child thinking about world peace. We don't have long to organize it all. Will you come to the next meeting? We need you, Jess.'

I can see the school playing fields bright with tents and marquees, fluttering with pennants, crammed with children singing, dancing, laughing. I can see painted faces and CND flags and white doves and a hundred home-made friendship bracelets tied on to wrists. We could change the way those kids think about the world. We could raise money, make a difference.

'Maybe,' I say.

'Thanks, Jess,' Miss Anderson grins. 'We need you, really. Bring Ellie and Jade and Lisa, but come along. Please.'

'OK.'

'Look, I didn't mean to keep you late,' Miss Anderson says. 'Better get away for your bus. I'll see you at that meeting, though, OK?'

'I'll be there.'

My mind is buzzing with ideas as I walk from the music room out towards the buses. When I reach the school gates I scrabble for my bus pass and that's when I realize I've forgotten my blazer, left it behind in the music room. I turn back, resigned, walk down across the courtyard and push open the swing door to the music room.

Jack's there.

He's sitting on a desktop, facing away from me, hunched over his guitar. Long fingers pick out the chords of a song I've never heard before, a song about a girl with faraway eyes.

My heart hammers as I creep forward to lift my blazer from the chair-back. He won't see me, he won't hear me. And then he turns, pushing back that choppy caramel fringe and grinning a soft, lazy grin meant just for me.

'Hello, Jess,' he says.

9

'Haven't seen you for a while,' Jack says, lowering his guitar. 'I've missed you, Jess.'

My cheeks flood with colour. 'Me?' I mumble idiotically. 'You've missed . . . me?'

'Yeah, course!' Jack grins. 'We're mates, aren't we? Kady said you two had fallen out. I'm sorry about that.'

'Well. People grow apart. Friends aren't always forever.'

Jack shrugs. 'I don't believe in forever,' he

says. 'It's a long, long time. Why make promises when you can live for the day?'

'Maybe.' I pick up the abandoned blazer, back away softly. Jack is looking at me a little too intently.

'Don't go,' he says. 'Sit down a minute. What's the rush?'

I take another step backwards, sit down on a desktop. 'No rush,' I whisper. 'I think I've missed my bus anyhow.'

'I'll walk you home.'

A few weeks ago, I'd have done anything to hear him say that. It's different now, of course. He's Kady's boy.

'So,' I say into the silence. 'How's the band?'

'Going great,' Jack tells me. 'We've really hit it off. Karl's amazing on drums, he really stirs the whole thing up. Alex knows exactly the sound I'm after on bass. And Lucie's really talented – she's a great girl. We're doing some songwriting together.'

'Right. Like that song you were playing when I came in?'

'That's one I'm working on myself,' Jack says. 'It's about a girl I really like ... someone I once thought I'd get to know a bit better.'

I swallow. 'And didn't you?'

'Not yet.'

'Well, I guess you've got Kady now,' I point out.

'Yeah. I've got Kady.' Jack stands up abruptly, slides his guitar into its case. 'Look, I'm not really in the mood for practising today. Why don't we just go?'

So we do.

We take the long way home, idling through the quiet streets, cutting through the park. Jack talks about Fallen Stars and his dreams of making it big some day. 'I want to be somebody,' he tells me. 'You know?'

'You *are* somebody, Jack.'

He rewards me with a flash of that soft, lazy grin. 'You always know how to make me feel good,' he says, and my heart starts up its hammer-beat again, too fast, too scary. Is this how Kady feels when she's close to him? Is this why she can't give him up?

'We're working so hard to be ready in time for the Peace Festival,' Jack continues. 'It's a brilliant opportunity. The press will be there, maybe even the TV. It could be our big break!'

'Hope so,' I tell him. 'You deserve it.'

A couple of little kids get off the swings up ahead of us, and Jack turns to me, grinning. 'Shall we?'

He grabs my hand and pulls me to the swings, and a voice in my head wonders what Kady would think about this, but Kady isn't here right now and I am. Jack's hand is wrapped around mine and it feels good. We jump on to the swings, kicking our legs, pushing ourselves upwards. My hair streams out behind me and I'm squealing, laughing, swinging higher and higher until I feel like I could fly.

It's Jack who does that, though, launching himself through the air in a great star-jump of gawky, black-clad limbs, laughing as he hits the grass and takes a bow to his imaginary audience.

'C'mon!' Jack shouts. 'Don't be a chicken! Jump, Jess! I'll catch you!'

I let myself slow, my legs dangling, and look down at Jack with his messy hair and his laughing eyes and his arms stretched out wide. And then I jump.

I land in his arms, the place I've wanted to be all along. I stagger against him, and we take a couple of steps backwards, laughing, and then he pulls me tight and he's kissing me, so softly, and I think my heart might just about burst with happiness.

Then it's over and I step back, blinking, frowning. 'What about Kady?' I say.

Jack grins and stretches his arms out, trying to reel me in, like I'm a fish he just caught and doesn't want to lose.

'I haven't made any promises to Kady,' he

says. 'It was you I liked first, Jess, you know that, don't you? It's OK.'

But it isn't OK. If Jack liked me first, then how come he's dating Kady? And if he's dating Kady, how come he's kissing me?

'This is wrong,' I whisper, and although my hands are shaking, I push him away. 'I don't want this.'

'Jess, wait . . .'

But I grab up my blazer and my rucksack and turn away from him, pulling out of his grasp when he tries to pull me back. He's the coolest, the cutest, the best-looking boy I've ever seen, but he's a boy who doesn't believe in forever, a boy who doesn't belong to me.

'Well, your loss,' Jack says, behind me. 'No need to tell Kady, OK?'

My loss? I guess it is.

IO

kady, i need 2 talk 2 u about jack. he's gonna hurt u. he's not honest. i'm sorry we quarrelled & i wanna make it rite, ok?
love, peace & chocolate,
jess xx

jess, i no u're jealous but u can't spoil this 4 me. jack & i r happy, so back off & leave us alone.
kady

It's the first time ever Kady's signed off a text without writing *love, peace & chocolate*. She must be really mad at me. It's not like I thought she'd be jumping for joy – who wants to be told their boyfriend's a loser? I just thought she'd agree to see me, hear me out.

Looks like I was wrong.

A football bounces past my feet, and Karl Williams runs over, scoops it up and kicks it back into the playground. He turns to me.

'You OK?' he asks.

I nod, but I'm not OK, not really. Fat, salty tears leak from the corners of my eyes and roll down across my cheeks. Karl hands me a folded white handkerchief, surprisingly clean.

'Wanna tell me?' he asks.

I shake my head, but Karl doesn't go away. He just sits beside me on the wall, silent, comforting.

'I've messed up,' I tell him at last.

'Is that all?' he asks. 'I've messed up more times than I can remember. You'll survive.'

'I won't,' I argue. 'I've lost my best friend.'

'Kady?' he says. 'How did that happen?'

My face crumples and I have to hide behind the handkerchief.

'Jack Somers?' Karl guesses, and I nod. I wipe my eyes, blow my nose.

'He's not worth it,' Karl says. 'Really.'

'How would you know?' I snap, lashing out because I'm hurting so much. 'How would you know how it feels to like someone who doesn't like you back?'

Karl shrugs and looks at me sadly. 'I do, OK?' he says. 'I just do.'

We sit in silence for a couple of minutes, and Karl takes a half-eaten Dairy Milk out of his blazer pocket and hands me a square. It helps, a bit.

'You're right,' I say in a tiny voice. 'About Jack Somers. He's not as nice as everyone thinks he is.'

'He's hopeless,' Karl agrees. 'He has an ego the size of a football pitch, and he's a born flirt. I've seen him in action – he was flirting with Miss Anderson the other day, and she has to be at least thirty!'

'But what about Kady?' I wail. 'She thinks he's Mr Perfect. She's going to get hurt, and there's nothing I can do to stop it!'

'Sometimes people have to make their

own mistakes,' Karl says. 'I know. I've made plenty!'

'You mean I just have to back off and let her get on with it?'

'Do you have another choice?'

'Not really.'

'Well, then,' Karl shrugs. 'It'll all work out in the end. Things usually do.'

He gets up and walks back towards the football game, then stops and turns, grinning. He throws the Dairy Milk bar through the air like a rounders ball, and I grab it, laughing.

'Supplies for later,' he tells me. 'I think you may need it more than I do!'

Walking into the meeting for the Parkway Peace Festival is the hardest thing I've ever done, even with Ellie, Jade and Lisa in tow. We sit down near the back, as far as we can get from Jack and Kady.

Miss Anderson is running the meeting, and the festival, pretty much. She starts off by saying how important the event will be. The school has picked out four charities to support, all of which work for peace in some way or another. The charities will each run a stall at the festival, telling people what they do, how they work, why they are needed.

'Our aim is to raise money for those charities,' Miss Anderson tells us. 'The more we can raise, the more they can do.'

'We need the papers and the TV there,' Jack says. 'We've got the primary schools coming, but TV could get us to a much wider audience. People could pledge money to the charities, even after the festival is over. Or we could ask businesses to sponsor us.'

Nobody points out that it'd also be great publicity for Fallen Stars. Am I the only one who can see what Jack's after?

Probably.

'Good one, Jack,' Miss Anderson nods. 'It's not just about publicity and raising money, though. We have to do more than that – we're raising awareness, too! Why are we here? What are we doing this for?'

There's an awkward silence, and Karl Williams says something about sheltering from the rain.

'Funny, Karl,' Miss Anderson says. 'But I think we're actually here because we believe in world peace.'

'We want to put an end to poverty,' Lisa calls out.

'An end to racism,' Kady pipes up.

'An end to hunger,' Mr Barrow suggests, which is funny, because he's at least sixteen stone and can't ever have been hungry in his life.

'No more war!' someone adds.

'No more pollution!'

'Equality for all!'

'That's right!' Miss Anderson says. 'Those are the things we want to change. How can we get people thinking about those things? How can we get them to care?'

'Songs,' Jack suggests from the front. 'Fallen Stars are writing a new set especially for the festival.'

'Excellent, Jack,' Miss Anderson beams.

'Music is a powerful media. There are lots of old songs we can use to put the message across, too.'

'A real festival would have more than one band,' Karl points out. 'Why don't we put posters up in case anyone else wants to do something?'

'Good thinking,' Miss Anderson agrees. 'What else?'

'What about asking the Home Economics department to do the food?' suggests Jade. 'We could have real festival food, veggie stuff, Indian stuff, fun stuff . . .'

'Helium balloons,' someone else says. 'We could all write a wish for peace on to a balloon, then let them loose at the end.'

'I like it!' Miss Anderson grins. 'A bit like

Buddhist prayer flags, but with a modern twist!'

'We could do prayer flags, too!'

'How about planting snowdrop bulbs on the banking?' Ellie chips in. 'They'll flower in the middle of winter, when everything else is dead. It'd be a message of hope – white for peace.'

Once we get started, there are ideas flying all over the place, more ideas than anyone could ever use. Miss Anderson has already organized stilt-walkers and jugglers and mime artists from the local College of Performing Arts. A Year Seven says her mum will come and do hair-wraps, and someone's big sister has volunteered to do henna tattoos.

I'd love to chip in my ideas too, but I can't

risk doing that in front of Jack and Kady. Instead, I write them down and hand the slip of paper to Miss Anderson after the meeting is over.

'Friendship bracelets?' she reads. 'A friendship chain? That's wonderful, Jess. Friendship is kind of basic, isn't it? Showing people we care. We couldn't have a peace festival without putting friendship in there somewhere.'

I just smile and nod and walk away. How come, if I know all the answers, I've managed to make such a mess of things? There's just no answer to that.

II

The day of the Parkway Peace Festival finally rolls round, and it's everything I imagined and more. The playing fields are littered with tents, marquees and endless rows of stalls, and at the far end a big stage has been set up with a huge, fluttering CND flag hanging behind it.

Karl's drumming workshop sends a rumble of thunder out across the site, and there's an acoustic music tent and even a chill-out zone.

Ellie and I spot Mr Barrow sprawled on a pink beanbag, listening to trance music.

There are workshops for making maracas, shakers, aboriginal-style rainmakers, and crazy xylophones made from dangling wine bottles filled with different amounts of water. There are kids making sculptures from old twigs and pine cones, kites from snipped-up bin bags, masks from papier mâché.

The art department have got everyone tie-dying squares of old white cotton every colour of the rainbow, then drying them in the sun and writing on a prayer. Parkway kids run around tying the squares on to twine, and finally a 300-metre run of prayer flags is hung around the perimeter of the playing fields.

'It's beautiful,' Ellie says. 'The wind catches up the prayers and takes them to where they're needed – it's an old Buddhist idea. Cool, huh?'

'Cool.'

Ellie and I are working as stewards, herding a bunch of kids from one of the seven primary schools that feed into Parkway all around the site. We take them to the drumming tent, the dance workshop, the face-painting stall, the friendship bracelet marquee. Ellie and I make bracelets and tie them on to each other's wrists, like a promise.

I make a bracelet for Kady, and slip it into my pocket. We haven't spoken for five weeks – that's a long time to be without your best friend. Jade and Lisa and Sian and Becca give me bracelets as well, and even Karl, and I realize that you can't have too many friends, even if you haven't got the one you really want.

Once we've helped the primary kids make their friendship bracelets, Ellie and I take them round the stalls, let them sample the veggie food laid on by the HE department. They try out the circus skills tent, listen to the storyteller and write a wish in marker pen on to a white helium balloon, to be released at the end of the festival.

I wish I was a ballerina, a kid in my group writes.

I wish there was no hunger and no war and I was rich enough to drive a yellow Ferrari, another scrawls.

Ellie writes something about an end to greed and war and racism. Me? I just wish I had my best friend back.

Jack gets his wish, anyhow. The newspapers are out in force, and so is the local TV station, which films kids from our group balancing on unicycles, signing petitions to save the whale and make poverty history. They film the prayer flags being hung up, interview kids painting a rainbow on the wall of the bicycle shed, test out lanterns made from old baked bean cans and hats made from felted woolly jumpers.

And when the music starts, the TV people are filming it all. There's an all-girl band from Year Seven who think they're Girls Aloud, a bunch of baby-goths from one of the primary schools who've painted their faces white with added spider webs and black lipstick. A couple of sixth-formers do an anti-war rap, and then some of the teachers show their age, dressing up in scary 70s flares to play covers of peace-protester musicians like Bob Dylan,

John Lennon, Donovan and other ancient hippy-dippy types.

Then it's time for Fallen Stars. Jack lopes on to the stage, Alex, Karl and Lucie close behind. They're all wearing tight CND T-shirts and faded hipster jeans, and they look casual, careless and very, very cool. Jack runs up to the mike.

'Thank you, everybody, for coming to the first ever Parkway Peace Festival!' he shouts, and the audience erupts like they've been waiting for this all day. Maybe they have. Jack rips into his first number, a crashing anti-war song that has everybody on their feet in seconds. Even the littlest kids are waving their arms in the air.

'He's good,' Ellie yells over the roar of the music.

Yeah, he's good – he's Parkway's very own rock star. When he looks out from under his raggedy fringe with those sparkly blue eyes, it feels like he's singing just for me, but I know better now than to believe that's true. Jack flirts with everybody – it's just the way he is.

Towards the end, the pace slows and Fallen Stars sing the song I heard Jack practising, about the girl with the faraway eyes. It's the song I thought he'd written for me, the song that fooled me into thinking he cared, but now that I listen properly I can see it's not about me at all. It's about a girl with faraway eyes in a far-off, war-torn land, who looks back to a time before the fighting started, and forward into the future to a time when the land will be at peace.

I was kidding myself all along.

The audience are swaying now, bodies pressed together, arms stretched up towards the blue summer sky. The song ends, and Jack and Alex and Karl and Lucie run to the front of the stage, throwing handfuls of silver stuff out into the audience, and suddenly, all around us, little stars are falling, drifting down on to our hair, our clothes, our outstretched hands.

12

The audience is breaking up, clumps of kids of all ages heading back up to the stalls, the tents, eager to squeeze the last dregs of fun from the day. I want to find Kady. What's the point of campaigning for peace, if I'm still fighting with my best friend?

'Will you be OK with the kids for a little while?' I ask Ellie. 'I need to find Kady.'

Ellie grins and tells me there's no problem, and I watch her head towards the stalls, ten blissed-out, face-painted, peace-loving primary kids trailing along behind her.

I turn the other way, head towards the stage, because wherever Jack is right now, that's where Kady will be too. I take a deep breath in, finger the narrow friendship bracelet in my pocket, the one I made for Kady. I have no way of knowing whether she'll take it. It'd serve me right if she threw it back in my face, but I'm hoping she won't.

If you want to make things right, say sorry, then a peace festival has to be as good a place as any to do it.

Backstage, kids are packing up equipment, unplugging amps and speakers.

'Has anyone seen Kady?' I ask.

'Think she's back there with Jack,' someone says.

So I pick my way further on, stepping over abandoned guitar cases and overturned mike stands, until I'm right back in the wings. And there, tucked behind the rack of lurid hippy-style costumes the teachers were wearing earlier, I see Jack. He has his arms around a girl, but the girl isn't Kady. It's Lucie, the keyboard-player from the band.

My instinct is to get out of there, and fast, but I back into the clothes rack and Jack looks up, right into my eyes.

'You,' he says, looking faintly hacked off.

'I'm looking for Kady,' I say. 'But she's not here, obviously.'

'Obviously,' Lucie says, smirking.

'She was,' Jack says regretfully. 'She left in kind of a hurry.'

'Kady *saw* you?' I echo. 'You and . . . *her*?'

"Fraid so,' Jack sighs. 'She was a bit upset.'

Lucie hooks her arm around Jack. 'It's best that she knows,' she whispers softly. 'Isn't it?'

Jack looks embarrassed. 'Maybe,' he shrugs.

I need fresh air. I turn and run out of the wings, down off the stage, away through the crowded, crazy festival that has invaded Parkway Community School. I push past jugglers, dodge around stilt-walkers, duck out of sight when Karl Williams waves at me through the crowd.

I need to find Kady, because if she saw what I saw, she's going to be crushed, distraught, devastated. She's going to need me.

Where would I go if I was falling apart, on a day like this when every centimetre of the school grounds is packed with people? Inside the school. It's out of bounds, except for the ground-floor toilets and the staff room, but Mrs Noble, who's meant to be guarding the doors, is down on the field having a henna tattoo painted on to her arm. I slip unchallenged into the silent corridors.

I find Kady, at last, in the girls' loos on the first floor, just next to our form room. The place seems empty enough, but one of the cubicle doors is closed, locked.

'Kady?' I call.

There's a gasping, snuffling sound from the other side of the door. 'Go away!' a muffled voice says.

'Kady?' I repeat. 'It's me, Jess. Open up, please!'

There's more snuffling, but finally the door

swings open. Kady is inside, huddled on the floor, arms around her knees, face to the wall. Her back shudders and trembles as each new sob tears through her, and my heart melts. I kneel down beside her on the cold lino, put my arms around her.

'It's OK, Kady,' I tell her. 'It's OK.'

And Kady turns and puts her head on my shoulder and cries and cries and cries until we've used up all the toilet tissue in the cubicle and used up all of Kady's hurt, all of her anger, all of her grief. Then we creep out of the cubicle and she splashes her blotchy, swollen face with cold water and I blot it dry for her with a paper towel.

'You were right,' she whispers. 'You were right about Jack. I suppose you're going to say *I told you so*?'

'No, I'm not,' I tell her. 'He had me fooled as well, remember?'

'Oh, yeah,' Kady says. 'You liked him too.'

'Mmm, I liked him too. But he wasn't right for either of us. He wasn't good enough for either of us.'

'He's gorgeous!' Kady protests.

'Dangerous,' I remind her. 'We thought we could handle it, but we got our fingers burnt.'

'Too right,' Kady says. 'I thought he'd make me happy, but he didn't. He went off with other girls, and said it didn't mean anything. Well, it meant something to me!'

'I know,' I say, stroking her hair.

'And he promised there was nothing going on with Lucie, but when I went backstage after the gig . . .'

'I know,' I repeat. 'He's not worth it. You'll get over him, Kady.'

'Will I?'

'Definitely.'

She grins at me, all big brown eyes and tear-stained cheeks. 'I've missed you, Jess. Seriously.'

'I've missed you too.'

I fish the friendship bracelet out of my pocket and hold it out, and Kady laughs out loud, that big, unruly giggle I haven't heard for so long.

'I made you one too!'

We tie the bracelets on to each other's wrists.

'Jack kept saying nothing was forever,' Kady says. 'But this is, OK? Friends forever.'

'Always,' I promise. 'And no boy is ever

going to get in the way of that again.'

'No chance,' Kady says. 'Not ever.'

Then she squints into the mirror, smooths down her braids and slicks a little eyeliner under each eye. 'Good as new,' she says. 'C'mon!'

'Where are we going?'

'To show Jack Somers he can't beat us!' Kady laughs, and we run down the staircase and through the quiet corridors and out on to the festival field.

Miss Anderson and Mr Barrow are organizing the final event, one huge, endless friendship chain, stretching right around the playing fields.

'Come on, girls!' Miss Anderson shouts, and then Ellie runs out of the chain and grabs Kady's hand, and Karl Williams leans forward and grabs mine, and Kady takes my other hand because nothing is going to separate us again, no way. The loudspeaker starts spouting out an ancient Beatles track, 'All You Need Is Love'.

'What is this drivel?' Kady squeals. 'My grandad plays this song!'

'It's cool,' Karl argues, and nobody smirks or rolls their eyes or asks Karl how he would know what was cool and what wasn't. Ellie and Karl pull us into the circle and the whole big chain of people starts moving round, slowly at first, then faster, like some crazy outsize hokey-cokey dance.

I catch sight of Jack and Lucie, and I try very hard to glare at them but I can't, I'm laughing, and Jack's laughing too, and I know there's no point blaming him because he's just a born flirt with an ego the size of a football pitch, like Karl said.

Lucie's welcome to him.

'This song is SO lame,' Kady says. 'Who needs love? Not me!'

But she's wrong about that, because there's more than one kind of love, and without it we just wouldn't be here. It's the glue that holds us all together.

'Love's OK,' I tell her. 'And peace . . .'

'And chocolate!' Kady makes as if to break the chain, but Ellie, Karl and I all screech at her not to, and she laughs and says she has M&M's in her pocket and we can all have some later, if we're good.

Then Miss Anderson runs into the middle of the circle and climbs on to a little makeshift stage, takes the mike. She thanks everybody for being here today, for making the festival such a success. She tells us that we've raised almost £6,000 for the charities we're supporting, but, more than that, we're making a difference, changing the way people think.

'They still haven't abolished maths homework, though,' Kady sulks, and everyone tells her to shut up.

Then Miss Anderson jumps down from the stage and loosens the nets that are holding down huge clouds of white wish-balloons from earlier on. The balloons float up, up into the clear blue sky and out over the rooftops of the town, higher and higher, and we watch and cheer and wave, shading our eyes from the sun, until the very last one is lost from sight.

BEST FRIENDS are there for you in the good times and the bad. They can keep a secret and understand the healing power of chocolate.

BEST FRIENDS make you laugh and make you happy. They are there when things go wrong, and never expect any thanks.

BEST FRIENDS are forever,
BEST FRIENDS ROCK!

IS YOUR BEST FRIEND ONE IN A MILLION?
Go to **cathycassidy.com**
to find out how you can show your best friend how much you care

Follow your dreams with all cathy cassidy's gorgeous books

A brand-new story and the first
in a gorgeous new series from

Cathy Cassidy

CHERRY CRUSH

COMING IN SEPTEMBER

the chocolate box girls

CHERRY — Dark almond eyes, skin the colour
of milky coffee, wild imagination, feisty, fun

*Each sister has a different story to tell,
which one will be your favourite?*

www.puffin.co.uk

Random Acts of
KINDNESS

Copy cool Sam Taylor from *Gingersnaps* and try a random act of kindness everyday. Here are a few to start you off . . .

- ♥ **WASH UP** without being asked
- ♥ **HUG** a friend!
- ♥ **TALK** to someone who's feeling lonely or left out
- ♥ **COMPLIMENT** a classmate on his/her appearance
- ♥ **SEND A CARD** to your BF for no reason at all
- ♥ **CARRY SHOPPING** for an elderly neighbour
- ♥ **PLAY** with your little bruv/sister – it's fun!
- ♥ **SMILE** – it's free, and it makes everyone feel good. Especially you!

And why not show your BFs how much you care by organizing something that you could do together? The most important thing is spending time with each other and having fun!

- ♥ **THROW A MINI PARTY FOR YOUR BEST FRIENDS** – you could all watch a DVD together, or make your own dream flags to hang in your room. Or maybe you could bake your own Angel Cakes!

- ♥ **HOLD A CAKE SALE** – once you've baked your yummy cakes, why not set up a stall to sell them? Maybe you could raise money for a charity that really means something to you.

- ♥ **INVITE YOUR FRIENDS TO A CLOTHES-SWAPPING PARTY** – you might not be in love with that sparkly top any more, but maybe one of your friends would look great in it. And you save money by not having to buy new clothes! Why not make it into a pamper party and spoil each other with some new hair looks?

For more ideas go to cathycassidy.com

Bright and shiny and sizzling with fun stuff . . .

puffin.co.uk

WEB FUN

UNIQUE and exclusive digital content!
Podcasts, photos, Q&A, Day in the Life of, interviews
and much more, from Eoin Colfer, Cathy Cassidy,
Allan Ahlberg and Meg Rosoff to Lynley Dodd!

WEB NEWS

The **Puffin Blog** is packed with posts and photos from
Puffin HQ and special guest bloggers. You can also sign up
to our monthly newsletter **Puffin Beak Speak**

WEB CHAT

Discover something new EVERY month –
books, competitions and treats galore

WEBBED FEET

(Puffins have funny little feet and
brightly coloured beaks)

Point your mouse our way today!

It all started with a Scarecrow.

Puffin is seventy years old.
Sounds ancient, doesn't it? But Puffin has never been
so lively. We're always on the lookout for the next big
idea, which is how it began all those years ago.

Penguin Books was a big idea from the mind of
a man called Allen Lane, who in 1935 invented
the quality paperback and changed the world.
**And from great Penguins, great Puffins grew,
changing the face of children's books forever.**

The first four Puffin Picture Books were hatched in 1940 and the
first Puffin story book featured a man with broomstick arms called
Worzel Gummidge. In 1967 Kaye Webb, Puffin Editor, started the
Puffin Club, promising to **'make children into readers'**.
She kept that promise and over 200,000 children became
devoted Puffineers through their quarterly instalments of
Puffin Post, which is now back for a new generation.

Many years from now, we hope you'll look back and
remember Puffin with a smile. **No matter what your age
or what you're into, there's a Puffin for everyone.**
The possibilities are endless, but one thing is for sure:
whether it's a picture book or a paperback, a sticker book
or a hardback, **if it's got that little Puffin
on it – it's bound to be good.**